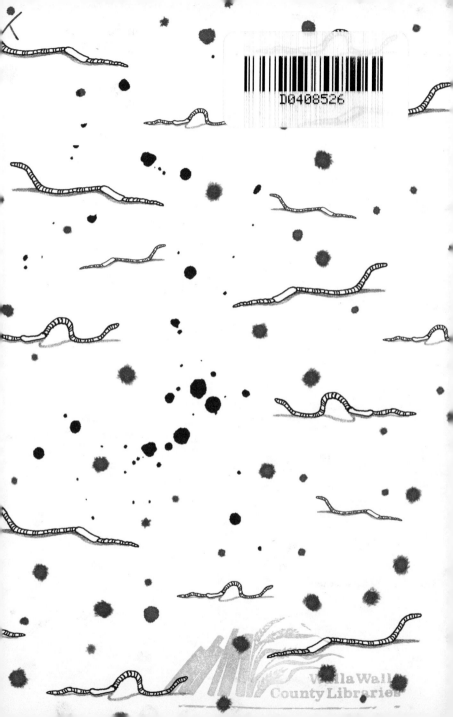

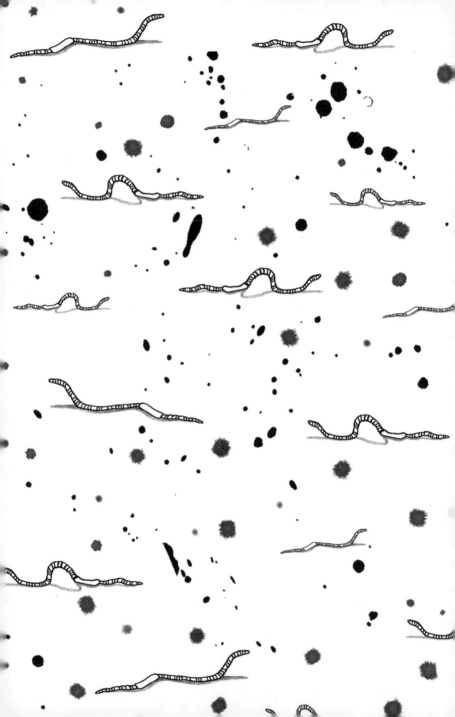

Dirty Bertie

WORMS!

DAVID ROBERTS

WRITTEN BY ALAN MACDONALD

CAPSTONE

First published in the United States in 2013
by Stone Arch Books
A Capstone Imprint
1710 Roe Crest Drive
North Mankato, Minnesota 56003
www.capstonepub.com

First published by
Stripes Publishing
1 The Coda Centre, 189 Munster Road
London SW6 6AW

Characters created by David Roberts
Text © Alan MacDonald 2006
Illustrations © David Roberts 2006

Library of Congress Cataloging-in-Publication Data is available
on the Library of Congress website.

ISBN: 978-1-4342-4619-6 (hardcover)
ISBN: 978-1-4342-4823-7 (paperback)

Summary: Bertie tries to get out of attending a pink party,
struggles to be polite for an entire day, and puts his green
thumb to the test in a flower-arranging competition.

Designed by: Kristi Carlson

Photo Credits
Alan MacDonald, pg. 112 ; David Roberts, pg. 112

Printed in the United States of America in Stevens Point, Wisconsin.
092012   006937WZS13

TABLE OF CONTENTS

WORMS!

CHAPTER 1

"Bertie, don't do that!" said his mom, looking up from her breakfast on Monday morning.

"Do what?" Bertie asked.

"Let Whiffer lick your spoon!" Mom said. "I saw you!"

"But he's hungry!" Bertie said.

"I don't care," Mom said with an exasperated sigh. "That's gross, Bertie."

Bertie inspected his spoon and gave it a lick. It looked clean enough to him.

Just then he heard the mail slide through the mail slot and hit the floor with a *THUNK!*

Bertie immediately jumped up from his seat at the table and ran down the hall. He hardly ever got something in the mail, but that didn't stop him from checking. He quickly flipped through the envelopes. Dad, Mom, Mom, Dad, boring, boring . . .

Wait a minute! There

was a letter with his name written on it in big, clumsy letters!

Bertie burst into the kitchen. "I got a letter!" he hollered, tearing open the envelope. The decorations on the card could only mean one thing — a party!

Bertie loved birthday parties. He loved the games, the cake, and especially the party favors. Last year he'd had a dog party, and everyone had come as a dog. Bertie had been a bloodhound with Dracula fangs. He'd wanted to have dog biscuits instead of cake, but his mom had put her foot down.

Mom picked up the invitation. "Oh, how fun, Bertie!" she said. "Angela invited you to her birthday party."

"Angela?" said Bertie. The smile

drained from his face. "Angela from next door!?"

"Of course Angela from next door," Mom said, shaking her head. "Who else?"

"Bertie's girlfriend!" his sister Suzy teased him.

Bertie snatched the invitation out of his mom's hand and read the message inside.

Please come to my pink birthday party on Friday! Don't forget to wear something pink!

love and kisses, Angela

Bertie's mouth dropped open. His whole body sagged with disappointment.

Angela Nunley lived next door and was almost six. She had long, straight blonde hair, rosy cheeks, and large blue eyes. Worst of all, she was totally in love with Bertie. She followed him around like a shadow.

He didn't want to go to Angela's party in the first place, and he definitely didn't want to go to a party where he had to wear pink. Bertie's favorite color was brown. Mud was brown, fingernails were brown, poop was brown. Ribbons, bows, and ballet shoes, they were pink.

"I don't have to go, do I?" asked Bertie.

"Nose, Bertie," said Mom.

Bertie removed a finger that had strayed up his nose.

"Angela invited you," said Mom. "How would you feel if you invited Angela to your party and she didn't come?"

"I'd feel happy," Bertie answered truthfully.

"It's a party, Bertie. You love parties," said Mom.

"And you love Angela!" Suzy taunted him.

Bertie ignored his sister. "It'll be terrible!" he said. "They'll all want to play princesses. Can't you say I have to go to the dentist or something?"

Mom gave him a look. "That would be a lie, wouldn't it, Bertie?" she said.

"Mom! It'll be all girls," Bertie complained. "I'll be the only boy there!"

"I'm sure it'll be fun," Mom said. "Now, I have to go. I'm late for work." She kissed him on the cheek and hurried out the door.

Bertie slumped into a chair.

A pink party with annoying Angela and her dumb friends — could things possibly get any worse?

CHAPTER 2

The next day, Bertie overheard
Mrs. Nunley talking to his mom about
Angela's birthday party. It was just as
bad as he'd thought. He was the only
boy invited — along with six of Angela's
girlfriends.

"Angela is so excited that Bertie is coming to her party," said Mrs. Nunley. "I think it's just so sweet that she's invited her little boyfriend."

Bertie almost threw up. Boyfriend? Gross! He wasn't Angela's boyfriend! If his friends ever heard about him going to a pink party they'd make fun of him for weeks!

I'm not going, and that's that, Bertie thought. *If Mom won't come up with an excuse, then I'll just have to think of one myself.* After all, when it came to excuses, Bertie was the best.

Bertie hurried up to his bedroom and dug beneath his bed to find the shoebox where he kept all of his top-secret possessions. He pulled out a notebook

and started writing a list of possible
excuses.

Brilliant Excuses for
Not Going to Angela's Party:

1. A crocodile bit my head off, and now I can't
   talk to anyone.

2. I have a rare disease called Party-itis which
   makes me break out in horrible spots.

3. I had baked beans for breakfast, lunch, and dinner. I think you know what that means.

4. I lost my memory. What party?

Bertie read back through his list. "Brilliant Excuse #4" would definitely work. Now all he had to do was talk to Angela and convince her. Then he would be off the hook. No stinky-pink party for him.

Bertie got his chance during lunchtime on Wednesday. He was eating with his best friends Darren and Eugene in the school cafeteria. All three boys were busy flicking peas at the next table to see who could get one down the back of Know-It-All Nick's sweater.

Angela suddenly appeared out of nowhere. "Hi, Bertie!" she said cheerfully.

Bertie stared at her blankly. "Who are you?" he asked.

Angela giggled. "You're so funny,

Bertie!" she said. "Did you get my invitation? You are coming to my party, aren't you?"

Bertie frowned at her. "Party?" he said. "What party?"

"You know, my pink party!" Angela told him.

"*Pink* party?" Darren repeated, cracking up. "Bertie's going to a *girl's* party!"

Bertie glared at his friend. "Sorry, I don't remember any party," he told Angela. "Maybe you didn't hear, but I lost my memory."

"What?" said Angela. "How?"

"I don't know. I can't remember," Bertie said, shrugging. "I must have hit my head or something."

"Oh, poor Bertie!" Angela said.

Eugene and Darren exchanged glances. "Poor Bertie!" they mimicked.

Angela reached out and put her hand on top of Bertie's. Bertie quickly pulled away.

"Never mind," she said. "The party is going to be at my house on Friday. We're having a bouncy castle."

"Have a nice time," said Bertie, loading more peas onto his spoon.

Angela stamped her foot. "You have to come, Bertie!" she said. "Laura and Missy are coming, and I told them you're my boyfriend."

Eugene started laughing so hard he fell off his chair. Bertie stared hard at Angela as if she looked faintly familiar.

"Sorry, what did you say your name was?" he asked.

Angela scowled at him and stormed off. Bertie let out a sigh of relief. It had been a close call, but his plan had worked.

No pink party for me, Bertie thought.

That night, Mrs. Nunley stopped by the house to talk to his mother. Sensing trouble, Bertie hid in his room. But as soon as the front door closed, there was a shout from downstairs.

"BERTIE!" Mom yelled. "Get down here! Right now!"

Bertie slunk downstairs.

"What is this I hear about you losing your memory?" she demanded.

Bertie stared at his feet. "Um . . . well . . . it just seems to keep . . . um . . . disappearing," he mumbled.

"Oh, really?" Mom said. "So you don't remember getting the invitation to Angela's birthday party?"

Bertie scrunched up his face and scratched his head. "What invitation?" he asked.

Mom folded her arms across her chest. "Well, that's too bad," she said. "That new pirate movie you wanted to see is playing this weekend. But you probably forgot about that too, didn't you?"

Bertie hadn't forgotten at all. *"Pirates of Blood Island!"* he blurted out. He'd been begging his mom to let him see that movie for weeks.

"Aha! So your memory is working after all," said Mom.

"I . . . um . . . well, I remember *some* things," Bertie admitted. "But other things I forget."

"Hmm," said Mom. "Well, don't worry because I made sure to mark Angela's party on the calendar to remind you."

She pointed to the calendar. The date of the party, Friday the 9th, was circled in red.

"Oh, and, Bertie?" Mom added.

"Yes?" Bertie said.

"I won't forget."

Bertie scowled and slunk out of the kitchen. He knew when he was beaten.

CHAPTER 3

Before Bertie knew it, it was Friday, the day of the party. After school, he went up to his room to play with his pet earthworm, Arthur. Arthur lived in a goldfish bowl that Bertie had filled with mud, leaves, and a plastic soldier for company.

Bertie was determined to train Arthur to come when he called him. "Arthur! Arthur!" he coaxed.

"Bertie!" Mom called from downstairs.

"Just a minute!" shouted Bertie, hiding the bowl under the bed. His mom didn't exactly know about Arthur yet.

A moment later, Mom poked her head around the corner and into his bedroom. "Hurry up, Bertie!" she said. "You're going to be late for the party."

"What party?" Bertie asked innocently.

"Nice try," Mom said. "But that's not going to work."

"But . . . but . . . I don't have a present for Angela," said Bertie desperately. "You can't go to a birthday party without a present!"

Mom held up two boxes. "The doll or the face paints?" she said.

Bertie sighed. "The face paints, I guess," he said gloomily. If he had to go to a pink party, he certainly wasn't going to show up with a doll.

"Oh, and I bought you this to wear." Mom said, handing him a brand-new T-shirt.

"Blech!" said Bertie. "It's pink. I can't wear that!"

"Don't be silly, Bertie. It's a pink party. Now hurry up and get ready." With that, Mom disappeared, leaving Bertie holding the pink horror.

Bertie retrieved Arthur's bowl from

underneath the bed. He held the T-shirt
up against his chest and looked in the
mirror.

"What do you think, Arthur?" he
asked. "Gross or what?"

Suddenly Bertie had the most
brilliant brainstorm. The invitation said
to wear something pink. Well, worms
were pink, weren't they? He could go

to the party as an earthworm! All he needed was something pink and wormy to wear.

Bertie tiptoed into his parents' room. Strictly speaking, he wasn't allowed to be in there. He'd been banned ever since the time he'd used Mom's favorite perfume to make a stink bomb. But what his parents didn't know wouldn't hurt them.

Opening the closet, Bertie started to pull out piles of clothes. Nothing pink there. But then — BINGO! On the top shelf, he spotted something pink. It was Suzy's sleeping bag, the one she was taking to summer camp. It was bright pink with a hood that fit snugly over your head.

That's perfect for an earthworm! Bertie thought. *It just needs a few finishing touches.*

Ten minutes later, Bertie's mom found him in the back garden.

"Oh, Bertie!" she cried. "No, Bertie!"

"What's the matter?" Bertie asked.

"You're filthy!" Mom said. "Look at you!"

Bertie scrambled to his feet and inspected his costume. He was impressively dirty. But that was the whole point of rolling around in a flowerbed!

"Earthworms are supposed to be muddy," he explained. "They live underground."

"Bertie!" Mom snapped. "I asked you to get ready for the party!"

"I am ready," Bertie insisted. "The invitation said I had to wear pink, so I am. I'm going as an earthworm."

Mom looked at him more closely. "What is that?" she asked. "It's not Suzy's sleeping bag, is it?"

"It sure is!" Bertie said with a grin. "It's perfect!"

The sleeping bag was smeared with mud. It covered Bertie from head to toe. Only his dirt-covered face peered out.

Mom sat down heavily on the ground. "Bertie, you can't go like that," she said.

"Why not?" Bertie asked. "It's pink. I bet no one else will be going as an earthworm."

"No," Mom said, sighing wearily. "I doubt they will."

CHAPTER 4

Angela's front door was covered with bright pink balloons when Bertie came hopping up the sidewalk like a giant pink jumping bean. Mom walked right up and rang the doorbell. Mrs. Nunley came to the door a second later.

"Hello!" she said cheerfully. Then she caught sight of Bertie. "Oh, goodness! What are you supposed to be?"

"I'm an earthworm," Bertie explained happily.

"How . . . uh . . . interesting, Bertie," said Mrs. Nunley. "Um, come on in."

Bertie hopped into the house, showering the clean carpet with clumps of dirt as he bounced into the living room.

Most of Angela's friends had come to the party dressed as princesses and fairies. The living room was a sea of pink tutus.

"You're here, Bertie!" said Angela, running up to him. "I'm a fairy. Look, I've got wings!"

"I'm an earthworm," said Bertie. "I got you a present."

An arm emerged from the sleeping bag holding a crumpled, messy-looking package. Angela quickly tore off the wrapping paper.

"Thank you!" she exclaimed, dropping the face paints on top of her big pile of presents. Bertie gazed at them longingly.

"Let's play a game," Mrs. Nunley said. "Who wants to play musical statues?"

"Me! Me!" the fairies and princesses all shouted eagerly.

Mrs. Nunley started the music, and all the party guests began dancing around the room.

"Bertie isn't dancing!" Angela complained.

"Yes, I am," said Bertie. "This is how earthworms dance!"

To prove his point, Bertie started rolling across the floor so that the dancing fairies and princesses had to jump over him. The music suddenly screeched to a stop.

"Statues, everyone!" Mrs. Nunley called out. "Statues!"

The dancing fairies and princesses all immediately turned into wobbling statues. But Bertie, who was feeling a little hot and dizzy from all his rolling, hadn't been listening. He just kept right on rolling . . . straight into one of the frozen fairies.

Laura wobbled and fell into Angela. Angela wobbled and fell on top of Missy

and Clare. Soon all the statues had
collapsed in a heap.

Bertie rolled to a stop at Mrs.
Nunley's feet. "Did I win?" he asked.

Mrs. Nunley sighed. That was the end
of the game. She herded all the guests
into the kitchen for cake and ice cream.

Everything was pink — pink plates,

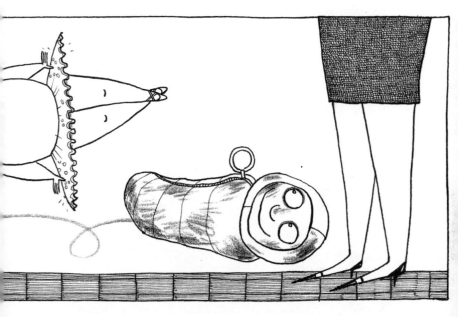

pink cups, pink ice cream, and a pink
heart-shaped birthday cake. Bertie ate
his cake worm-style, licking things off
his plate.

"Bertie, please don't slurp your food
like that," Mrs. Nunley said, giving him
a pointed look.

"Sorry," Bertie replied. "Worms

can't help it. They don't know about manners."

When everyone was done eating, Mrs. Nunley looked around at the mess on the floor. Most of it had collected under Bertie's chair.

"Can we go in the bouncy castle now?" Bertie asked.

"In a minute, Bertie!" Mrs. Nunley said. "Angela, why don't you all go into the other room and play with your presents?"

While Angela's friends played with her Little Patty Pony set, Bertie eyed the face paints.

Maybe I can just try one of them, he thought. Bertie wriggled one arm out of his sleeping bag and picked up the black face paint. He used it to draw on his chin, then looked in the mirror. Next he drew on his cheeks. Maybe he would turn himself into a vampire or a zombie!

Bertie was so busy working that he didn't notice the rest of the room had gone quiet. He looked up to find all the princesses and fairies staring at him.

"What are you doing?" Angela asked.

"Ah, sorry," said Bertie, "I was just . . . um . . . borrowing them."

"What have you done to your face?" Angela asked.

"I'm a slug," said Bertie.

"You said you were a worm," she reminded him.

"I was, but now I'm a slug," Bertie said. "A big black slimy slug."

He slithered onto the floor, making slimy, sluggy noises. Angela's friends shrieked with delight and ran to hide behind the curtains. Angela peeped out, her eyes shining. "Make me a slug too, Bertie," she pleaded.

Mrs. Nunley was still trying to clean up when the doorbell rang. Thank goodness it was over for another year. When she answered the door, Bertie's mom stood on the doorstep with three other parents.

"I hope Bertie behaved himself," Bertie's mom said.

"Oh, he's such a . . . lively boy," Mrs. Nunley said. She led the parents through the house to the back door. "Everyone is playing in the back. Angela's had such a good time. They've all been good as . . ."

Mrs. Nunley suddenly came to a dead stop. In the backyard, eight children were bouncing on the bouncy castle. But the princesses and fairies who had come to the party had vanished. In their

place were ugly green monsters in filthy
tutus who looked like they'd crawled
from a swamp. Smack in the middle
of the group was Bertie, bouncing and
laughing.

"Look, Mom!" Angela called out. "I'm
a creepy caterpillar! Bertie did it!"

Mrs. Nunley looked at Bertie's mom.
The other parents looked at Bertie's
mom. Bertie's mom looked at Bertie.

"What?" said Bertie.

Back in his room, Bertie was glad
to be reunited with Arthur. He didn't
understand why everyone had been so

upset. What was the point of giving someone face paints if they weren't allowed to use them?

"I don't think they'll be inviting me next year," he told Arthur with a smile.

Bertie thought for a second. All in all, the party hadn't turned out so badly.

He reached into his pocket and pulled out something pink and sticky.

"Look, Arthur!" Bertie said. "I saved you some cake!"

MANNERS!

CHAPTER 1

Bertie had no manners — and everyone knew it. He fidgeted and fiddled and talked with his mouth full of food. He sniffed and slurped and burped and picked his nose.

"Bertie, use a tissue!" his mom was always telling him.

"Bertie, get your elbows off the table!"
his dad constantly said.

"Don't touch that, Bertie, it's dirty!"
his parents moaned every day.

But Bertie didn't see the point. Did
pigs or dogs have manners? No way!
When his dog Whiffer peed on a tree,
no one seemed to care. But if Bertie had
done that, his mom would have fainted
on the spot.

In Bertie's opinion, manners were a
total waste of time. But that was before
he heard about the prize.

Bertie's principal, Miss Skinner, was

the one who announced the prize during
an assembly in the school gym one
morning.

"Does anyone know what tomorrow
is?" she asked. Her gaze fell on Bertie,
who was busy crossing his eyes and
making funny faces at Darren.

"Bertie!" she said.

"Uh . . . yes, Miss Skinner?" Bertie
replied.

"Do you know what tomorrow is?"
Miss Skinner asked.

Bertie thought about it for a minute.
"Tuesday?" he guessed.

Miss Skinner gave him one of her
looks. "Tomorrow," she said, "is National
Manners Day. It's a day when we should
all be extra polite, so I want everyone

to think about their manners. We're lucky to have Miss Prim from the public library coming to visit us, and she has agreed to give a very special prize to the student with the best manners."

"A special prize!" Bertie said to Darren as they trooped back to their classroom. "I bet it's some boring old book about being polite."

"Actually, it's not," said an annoying voice from behind them. It was Know-It-All Nick, Bertie's worst enemy.

"How do you know?" asked Bertie.

"Because I heard Miss Skinner talking to Miss Boot," said Nick, looking pleased with himself. "She said the tickets arrived this morning."

"Tickets for what?" asked Darren.

"Wouldn't you like to know!" Nick said. The truth was, Nick would have liked to know himself.

"I bet it's tickets to a football game!" said Darren.

"Or movie tickets," said Donna, another girl in their class.

"Or tickets for Mega Mayhem," Bertie added, his eyes lighting up. Mega Mayhem was the best amusement park in the whole entire world, and he'd been begging to go for months.

"It doesn't matter what it is," Nick said smugly, "because I'm going to win. My mom says I have the best manners of anyone she's ever met."

"Well, too bad your face is so ugly," Bertie muttered.

Bertie thought about the prize for the rest of the day. He was sure the tickets were for Mega Mayhem and he'd made up his mind to win them. Even if it meant he had to be polite for a whole day, he didn't care. After all, how hard could it be?

CHAPTER 2

The next morning Bertie leaped out of
bed. Today was National Manners Day
— the day he was going to win the prize.
In the hallway, he ran into his mom,
who was coming out of the bathroom.

"Good morning, Mother," he said cheerfully. "Isn't it a beautiful morning?"

His mom gave him a suspicious look. "What did you do, Bertie?" she asked.

"I didn't do anything," said Bertie. "I was just being polite."

Downstairs, Dad and Suzy were eating breakfast.

"Good morning!" Bertie greeted them as he sat down at the table. He poured some cereal into his bowl and cleared his throat. "Ahem. Excuse me, Suzy. Would you be so kind as to pass me the milk, please?"

Suzy stared at him. "Why are you talking so funny?" she asked.

"It's not funny," he told his sister. "It's called being polite, thank you very much. Maybe you should try it some time."

Bertie carefully poured milk into his bowl without spilling a drop and ate his cereal as quietly as possible. Even when he dropped his spoon on the floor, he was careful to wipe it on his sweater before putting it in his mouth.

"I might be getting a prize today," he announced.

Dad glanced up from reading the newspaper. "Mmm? What kind of prize?" he asked.

"For being polite," said Bertie. "It's National Manners Day, and they're giving a prize for being polite."

"You? Polite? HA!" Suzy snorted with laughter.

Bertie glared at her. "I'm more polite than you, fat-face," he snapped.

"Bertie, be nice to your sister," said Dad. "And your nose is running. Use a tissue."

Bertie pulled a crumpled tissue out of his pocket and wiped his nose. Something fell out and plopped into the sugar bowl.

"Ewwww!" Suzy yelled. "What is that thing?"

"It's just Buzz. He won't hurt you," said Bertie, picking the big black fly out of the sugar bowl.

"Bertie! That's a dead fly!" Dad yelled.

"I know," replied Bertie. "Don't worry, I'm going to bury him."

Bertie had discovered Buzz dead

on his windowsill the other day. He'd
decided to bury him under the apple tree
in the backyard. It seemed like the polite
thing to do. Bertie picked Buzz up and
blew off the sugar that was stuck to his
wings.

"Throw that thing away!" said Dad. "It's disgusting!"

Bertie sighed and wrapped Buzz back up in his tissue. He would bury him after school.

That's what I get for trying to be polite, Bertie thought. *I do something nice, and all I get is people shouting at me.*

CHAPTER 3

Miss Prim, the local librarian, stood at the front of the class. She was tall and thin with glasses that hung around her neck on a cord.

Bertie had seen Miss Prim at the library. She stood behind a desk and helped people check out books.

He thought she must be at least a
hundred years old. He hoped she didn't
remember him. The last time he'd
gone to the library, Whiffer had done
something smelly in the corner. They'd
had to leave quickly.

"Class, this is Miss Prim," Miss Boot
said. "I hope we're all going to show her
how well-behaved we can be."

Miss Boot looked out over her class.
All the students were sitting up straight
and paying attention. It was amazing the
effect a prize could have. Even Bertie
looked interested, rather than slouched
over or sticking a pencil up his nose.

Miss Prim stepped forward and
started lecturing the class about the
importance of good manners. Bertie

tried to listen, but his mind kept drifting off. He was already imagining himself whizzing down the Slide of Doom at Mega Mayhem.

"Now," said Miss Boot, "who would like to show Miss Prim around the school? I need two volunteers."

Bertie immediately shot his hand into the air. This was his chance to show Miss Prim how polite he could be! Unfortunately everyone else in his class had the same idea. Thirty children strained out of their seats, waving their

hands in the air and shouting "Pick me! Pick me!"

Miss Boot pointed to Know-It-All Nick. "Nick," she said. "I'm sure you can lead our visitor on her tour."

Bertie couldn't believe it. Not Know-It-All Nick!

Why does he always get picked? Bertie thought angrily. *Just because he made Miss Boot a stupid card for her birthday. It's not fair! I never get picked for anything.*

Miss Boot hesitated. She needed someone else polite and reliable.

"Miss Boot, pick me!" the students pleaded. "Please, Miss Boot! I'll do it! Pick me!"

"What about that boy at the back?"

Miss Prim suggested. "The one who's sitting so quietly."

"Oh," said Miss Boot. "Bertie."

Bertie, who hadn't been listening, looked up. "Me?" he said.

Miss Prim walked down the hallway, admiring the paintings on the walls.

"That one's mine," said Nick proudly, pointing to a bright picture of a sunset.

"And that one's mine," Bertie said. He pointed to a splotchy mess of green paint. "It's an alien. And that's his dinner inside him."

"Oh," said Miss Prim. "How . . . um, unusual. Do you have a tissue, Bertie?"

"Oh, sure," Bertie said. He pulled a dirty tissue from his pocket and held it out it to Miss Prim.

"No, I meant for yourself," Miss Prim said. "You need to wipe your nose!"

"Oh, thanks," said Bertie. He wiped his nose on his sleeve and stuck the tissue back in his pocket. Buzz was still wrapped inside, and he didn't want him falling out.

Miss Prim sighed heavily. "Maybe we should head to the next classroom," she suggested.

Nick started to walk ahead quickly toward the next classroom. Bertie kept up with him. They both ran for the door and grabbed the handle at the same time.

"I was here first!" Know-It-All Nick said, yanking on the door.

"No, I was!" Bertie insisted.

Miss Prim caught up with them. "Boys! I hope we're not arguing," she said. "That's not very polite."

"Oh, no," Nick said with a smile.  "Of course not. I was just telling Bertie that his shirt is untucked."

Bertie glanced down at his shirt. Just then, Nick yanked the door open, squashing Bertie behind it.

"After you, Miss Prim," Nick said, holding the door open for the librarian.

Miss Prim smiled at him gratefully. "Thank you, Nicholas," she said. "It's nice to see that *someone* remembers their manners."

CHAPTER 4

By lunchtime, Bertie was exhausted.
Being polite was hard work, especially
with Know-It-All Nick trying to outdo
him the whole time. And now it looked
like he was stuck with Miss Prim for
lunch.

As they walked into the lunchroom,

Bertie could hardly believe his eyes.
No one in the lunch line was pushing
or shoving. There was no running or
fighting or throwing food across the
room. Everyone was eating their lunch
quietly and politely.

"Hello, Miss Prim!" Donna called as
they passed by.

Bertie gulped. Three of his teachers
were waiting for them at a table set with
a white tablecloth and a vase of flowers.

"Come and join us over here, Miss
Prim," Miss Skinner said. "Bertie will go
get your lunch."

"Hope you don't drop it, Bertie!"
Know-It-All Nick whispered.

"You'd better hope I don't drop it on
you," Bertie muttered.

Bertie took a seat across from Miss Prim and Know-It-All Nick and stared down at the plate in front of him. How was he supposed to eat spaghetti without making a mess?

He watched as Miss Prim wound spaghetti around her fork and tried to copy her. The spaghetti fell off before it reached his mouth.

Know-It-All Nick put a hand over his mouth and loudly sucked up a piece of spaghetti. *SHLOOOOOOOP!*

"Bertie!" Nick said. "Don't be so disgusting!"

The teachers all turned to look in Bertie's direction.

"But . . . but it wasn't me!" Bertie stuttered. "It was him!"

Miss Prim shook her head in disapproval. "Bertie, it isn't nice to lie," she scolded him.

Bertie turned to glare at Nick. He would have liked to put spaghetti down Nick's shirt. He would have liked to pour a glass of water down Nick's pants. But he wanted that prize, and Miss Prim was watching him like a hawk.

Bertie sighed and lifted his forkful of spaghetti to his mouth. Suddenly a hand reached out and smacked his elbow.

SPLAT! Spaghetti sauce landed on the white tablecloth.

"Oh, Bertie, you're so messy!" Nick said, smirking at him. "Look what you did!"

Miss Prim shook her head again.

"But it wasn't ME!" shouted Bertie.

Miss Boot glared at him. Bertie glared at Nick. He was going to get that two-faced slimy sneak.

After everyone finished eating, Nick went to get dessert. When he came back to the table, Bertie's eyes lit up. Chocolate fudge cake — his favorite! He reached out to grab a piece.

"Manners, Bertie," Miss Prim reminded him. "We don't grab, we offer the plate to others."

Bertie reluctantly passed the cake around the table. Miss Skinner took a slice, followed by Miss Boot and Mr. Plumly, the English teacher. Bertie watched anxiously as the cake began to disappear.

"Oh, dear," said Miss Prim, helping herself to a piece. "There's only one piece left! Which of you is going to have it?"

Bertie looked at Nick. Nick looked at Bertie. Both of them eyed the last slice of fudge cake. Then Nick did a surprising thing. He offered the plate to Bertie.

"You have it, Bertie," he said with a sickly sweet smile. "I insist."

Bertie wasn't going to fall for that one. "That's okay, Nick," he said. "You go ahead. I want you to have it."

"Well, if you insist," said Nick. "I wouldn't want it to go to waste." He snatched the last piece of cake and took a large bite. "Thanks, Bertie."

Bertie glared at Nick furiously. He'd been tricked!

That's it, Bertie thought. *No more manners. This means war.* That fudge cake was his, and he was going to get it back.

Bertie reached into his pocket and pulled out his tissue. Nick was too busy talking to Miss Prim to notice a hand darting across the table.

Any second now, thought Bertie. *Five, four, three, two . . .*

Nick reached for the cake and raised it to his mouth. There was something black on top.

"ARGHHHHH! A fly!" screamed Nick, dropping the cake on the table.

"ARGGHHHH!" shrieked Miss Prim as Buzz landed in front of her.

"I'll get it!" cried Miss Skinner. She grabbed a spoon and attacked the dead fly with a vengeance.

SMACK! WHACK! THUMP! Plates and cups leaped in the air. Buzz hopped

and jumped with each blow, showing surprising speed for a dead fly.

Miss Boot grabbed the water jug and emptied it over the table. *SPLOOSH!*

Buzz lay still in a puddle with his legs in the air.

"Is it dead?" asked Miss Skinner. She picked the fly up by one leg and examined it.

A loud burp broke the silence.

Six pairs of eyes turned to stare at Bertie. He had cake crumbs around his mouth and a satisfied smile on his face.

"Bertie!" Miss Skinner yelled. "What in the . . ."

"Um . . . excuse me!" Bertie said politely. He held out his hand. "Could I have my fly back, please?"

Later that afternoon, Bertie crowded into the auditorium with everyone else. The time had come for Miss Prim to announce the winner of the prize.

Bertie knew he didn't stand a chance after all the trouble at lunchtime. But at least he'd been able to rescue Buzz from the garbage. Besides, it had all been worth it to see the look on Know-It-All Nick's face when he'd come eye to eye with Buzz.

Bertie didn't mind who won — as long as it wasn't Nick.

"And the winner," Miss Prim announced from the podium, "is Nicholas Payne."

Bertie groaned. Know-It-All Nick
made his way up to the stage and shook
Miss Prim's hand. Everyone waited to
see what his prize would be.

Miss Prim smiled at Nick and handed
him an envelope. "Since you're always
so polite, I'm sure you're going to love
this prize," she told him. "It's two tickets
to the Museum of Manners."

Nick's face turned white and his
mouth dropped open. His mouth gaped
open but nothing came out.

Bertie leaned
forward in his seat.
"Manners, Nick,"
he called out.
"Aren't you going
to say thank you?"

CHAPTER 1

RUMBLE! RUMBLE! SCREECH! SNORT!

Something was making a lot of noise outside Bertie's window. Bertie yawned and rolled over in bed. Then he realized something. It was Saturday, his favorite day of the week. Saturday was garbage day!

Bertie sat straight up and pulled back his curtains. Sure enough, the garbage truck was at the far end of the street. If he hurried, he might still make it.

He found Mom in the kitchen making coffee.

"Morning, Ber . . ." Mom started to say. She broke off and stared at him. "What on earth are you wearing?"

Bertie looked down at his outfit. He was wearing his dad's painting overalls, a wool hat, and a muddy pair of boots. True, the overalls were a little too big, but Bertie thought they were perfect for a garbage man.

"It's Saturday," Bertie explained. "I have to go help Ed with the garbage."

"Oh, Bertie, not today," Mom said with a sigh.

"Why not?" Bertie asked.

"We're going to the fair this morning," Mom said. "I don't want you getting all dirty before we have to leave."

"That's why I'm wearing these!" said Bertie, flapping his long sleeves.

"Besides, you're too late," Mom said. "I took the trash out last night."

"But I always do it!" cried Bertie.

"I'm sorry, Bertie. I forgot," Mom said. "You can do it next time."

Bertie stared after his mom as she disappeared upstairs with her coffee.

Bertie looked down at Whiffer, who was lying on the floor, chewing on his bone. "How could she forget?" Bertie asked. "I always take the trash out on Saturdays!"

When he grew up, Bertie had decided he wanted to be a garbage man. He wanted to wear an orange jacket and big gloves and ride around in a truck that snorted like a dragon. Most of all he wanted to work with mountains of messy, smelly, sticky garbage.

Bertie loved garbage. He had piles of

it under his bed. String, Popsicle sticks, rubber bands, candy wrappers — he couldn't believe the stuff some people threw away!

Bertie started digging through the kitchen cabinets. The garbage man would be here any minute! Finally he found what he was looking for — a big black trash bag. Now all he needed was some garbage to fill it.

Bertie started grabbing things from around the kitchen. He tossed in a dish towel, a bar of soap, a can of cat food, and a pile of letters from his school — no one ever read them anyway. In went his dad's slippers, some carrots (yuck!), a head of cauliflower (double yuck!), and his sister's horse magazine.

RUMBLE, RUMBLE! The garbage truck was getting closer. Bertie hurried into the hallway, dragging his garbage bag behind him. Someone had left a pot of old flowers sitting next to the front door, just waiting to be thrown out. Bertie scooped them into the bag with the rest of the trash and hurried outside.

The garbage can was already at the curb, waiting to be picked up. Bertie climbed up on the front wall so he could drop his bag in.

Peering inside, Bertie caught sight of something familiar in one corner. Wait a minute . . . was that his chewing gum collection? Surely his mom hadn't thrown it out!

Bertie leaned over into the can to rescue it. The jar was just out of reach. He'd have to . . .

"ARGHHH!" Bertie yelled, toppling headfirst into the can. His face was wedged

against something soft and squishy.
"Mmff! Help!"

"Having some trouble?" a voice asked.
Strong hands pulled Bertie out of the
garbage can and set him on his feet.

"Uh-oh!" Ed the garbage man said
with a grin. "I don't think your mom is
going to be very happy with you, Bertie."

Bertie inspected himself. He did
seem to have gotten a little messy. There
was something sticky on his overalls
that smelled like ketchup. He brushed
off some tea leaves off his sleeve and
straightened his hat. A piece of potato
peel fell off. He held up the rescued jar
to show Ed.

"I was looking for this. It's my
chewing gum collection," Bertie

explained. "I'm doing an experiment to see what happens when it gets really old."

"And what have you learned so far?" Ed asked.

"That it gets really hard and tastes really disgusting," said Bertie. "Want to try some?"

"Not today, thanks," Ed said. "I have to get moving with this garbage. Want to give me a hand?"

"Yes, please!" said Bertie. "I brought you an extra bag today." He handed Ed the garbage he'd collected.

Ed dropped the bag into the wheeled trash can, and Bertie pulled it to the waiting truck. He watched in awe as the truck opened its metal jaws and swallowed up the garbage. Ed held out a gloved hand, and Bertie shook it.

"Good work," said Ed. "See you next week." He moved off down the road, whistling.

"See you later!" called Bertie.

CHAPTER 2

Back inside the house, Bertie whistled to himself as he scooped dog food into Whiffer's bowl. He whistled as he took off his overalls and sat down to have some breakfast.

"Bertie, please!" said Dad. "Could you not do that?"

"What?" said Bertie. "I'm just whistling."

"That isn't whistling," Dad said. "You sound like leaky balloon."

"Well, I have to practice," said Bertie. "How can I learn to whistle if you don't let me practice?"

Just then, Mom came into the kitchen looking frustrated. "Bertie, have you seen my flower arrangement? I left it by the front door this morning."

Bertie paused with his finger in the peanut butter. "By the door?" he asked.

"Yes, it's for the gardening competition at the summer fair," Mom said. "I spent hours working on it, and now I can't find it anywhere. Are you sure you haven't seen it?"

"Me? Um . . . no," Bertie said.

"Are you okay?" Mom asked. "You look a little pale."

"I'm fine," said Bertie. But the truth was, he suddenly wasn't feeling so well. He remembered the pot of old flowers by the front door. He remembered putting it in his garbage bag. Then he remembered the garbage truck eating it.

Uh-oh, Bertie thought. Now that he thought about it, he remembered his mom going on and on about the competition for weeks. Mrs. Nunley always won first place, but this year Bertie's mom felt like she had a real shot at winning. Or at least she would have . . . if Bertie hadn't thrown out her competition entry.

How was I supposed to know the flowers by the door were hers? he thought. *They looked practically dead!*

Bertie got up from the table and walked innocently toward the front door.

"Where are you going?" asked Mom. "You haven't finished your breakfast."

"I just need to do something," Bertie replied.

"What is all over Dad's overalls?" Mom asked, holding up the stained clothes Bertie had worn to take out the trash.

"Just some ketchup," Bertie said. "I might have had a little bit of an accident."

"Bertie!" Mom yelled.

But Bertie was already headed out the door. If he was going to get those flowers back, he needed to move fast.

CHAPTER 3

Bertie bent over the handlebars of his bike, pedaling as fast as he could. Whiffer raced along beside him, trying to keep up.

What if I'm already too late? Bertie worried as he raced along. Even if he caught up with the garbage truck, how was he going to get the flowers back? Ed had told him all the garbage trucks took their loads to an enormous dump.

Maybe Ed will let me hunt through the mountains of trash there, Bertie thought hopefully. He loved that idea. But when he reached the end of the road, there was no sign of Ed or the garbage truck. It could be miles away by now!

Bertie sped toward the park and slammed on his brakes at the corner. There, parked at the corner, was the garbage truck.

"Hey!" called Bertie. "Hey, wait a minute!"

The truck started to pull away. As Bertie watched, it picked up speed, turned a corner, and disappeared from

sight. Bertie looked down at Whiffer,
whose ears drooped in sympathy.

He was done for. Mom would scream.
Dad would shout. And he would be sent
to his room for a million years.

"Bertie, is that you?" Mom called as
he crept in through the front door.

"No," answered Bertie.

"I want a word with you," Mom said
sternly. "Now."

Bertie shuffled into the kitchen where
Mom, Dad, and Suzy were all waiting
for him. He could tell by their faces that
he was in trouble.

"Where are my slippers?" Dad asked.

"And where is my *Horse Weekly* magazine?" asked Suzy.

"And what have you done with my flower arrangement?" Mom demanded.

"Me?" Bertie said. "Why do I always get blamed? It's not my fault if people keep losing things!"

Mom folded her arms across her

chest and glared at him. "Look at me, Bertie," she said. "I want you to tell me the truth. Did you touch those flowers?"

Bertie looked down at his feet. "I might have um . . . given them to someone," he mumbled.

"I told you he did it!" Suzy exclaimed.

"To who?" Mom asked.

Bertie tried to think of an answer. He wanted to tell the truth, but the truth was he'd given the flowers to a garbage truck. By now they were probably buried under six feet of dirty diapers.

"I gave them to . . . um . . . to Gran!" he said with sudden inspiration.

"Gran?" Mom repeated, looking confused. "What on earth for?"

"She likes flowers," said Bertie. "She likes smelling them and stuff."

Mom looked unconvinced. "And when did you do this?" she asked.

"This morning," said Bertie. "I saw them by the front door, and I thought I'd take them to Gran to cheer her up."

His family stared at him suspiciously. Bertie had never given flowers to anyone before. On the other hand, he had been known to do all sorts of weird things.

Mom's expression softened a bit. "That was a nice thought, Bertie, but I need those flowers back," she said. "They have to be at the fairgrounds by ten. I'll call Gran."

Mom picked up the phone and started to dial.

"No!" Bertie exclaimed desperately. "I'll just go over there! It'll be faster that way. She's probably finished smelling them by now."

Mom set the phone back down. "All right, but you'd better hurry," she told him. "If I miss this competition you're in big trouble."

Bertie set off for Gran's house with Whiffer padding along beside him. At the end of the street, he sat down on a

wall to think. Now what was he going
to do? Bringing Gran into it had only
made things worse. Now Mom expected
him to come back with her stupid flower
arrangement.

Bertie stared gloomily
at Whiffer who was busy
sniffing around the
garden behind him.
The house was
empty and the
front yard was
overgrown with
tall weeds.

Suddenly Bertie had a
brilliant idea. He could make his own
flower arrangement! It would be easy!
There were hundreds of flowers right

here that nobody wanted. All he had to do was pick a handful, stick them in a vase, and enter it in the competition. If he took it to the fair himself, his mom would never find out.

Half an hour later, Bertie had put his plan into motion. The new flower arrangement had been safely delivered to the fair. He hurried home to tell his mom the good news.

CHAPTER 4

The fair was in full swing when Bertie and his family arrived. He wandered around the different booths with Whiffer on his leash. There were people selling plants and homemade jams, but nothing interested Bertie.

For some reason, Whiffer kept

whining and pulling him back to the table with all the flower arrangements.

Mrs. Nunley was standing at the table, talking to Bertie's mom. "I don't know what I'd do if I won again," she was saying. "It would be too embarrassing."

"I can imagine," Bertie's mom replied stiffly. She motioned to the table. "So which one is yours?"

"Oh, that little vase of tiger lilies," Mrs. Nunley replied, pointing to a towering display of yellow blooms. She lowered her voice and pointed to another vase. "Can you believe someone actually entered that mess?"

Bertie stared at the "mess" Mrs. Nunley was pointing at. It was a cracked vase full of dandelions, grass, and twigs, all sticking out in different directions. In the middle was what looked like a dog's bone.

"Actually," Bertie said loudly, "I think that's the best one."

Mom pulled him to one side. "Bertie, where is my flower arrangement?" she muttered. "I thought you said you turned it in."

"Um . . . I did," said Bertie. Luckily, one of the judges chose that moment to interrupt.

"Excuse me. Can I have everyone's attention? We're about to announce the results of the flower arranging competition," he boomed.

The judge started reading the list

of winners. Second place went to Mrs. Nunley, who tried her best not to look disappointed. First place went to Mr. Pye's display of roses.

"And finally," said the judge, "the prize for the most original display. This year we felt one entry beautifully captured our theme of 'Wild Nature.'"

The judge held up the vase full of dandelions and twigs. It was Bertie's entry. "The winner," he said, "is Mrs. Burns."

"That's us!" Bertie shouted excitedly.

Whiffer barked and pulled on his leash, trying to reach his bone, which sat in the center of the arrangement.

Mom looked at Bertie, then in horror at the vase of weeds the judge was holding. "Bertie, that is not my flower arrangement," she hissed.

"No," admitted Bertie. "I had to make a few . . . um . . . changes."

"Go," Dad whispered to Mom. "Everyone is waiting."

Mom reluctantly stepped forward to collect her prize. Her face was a deep shade of pink.

"I'm curious," the judge said. "What gave you the idea to use a dog bone? It's so original."

Mom shot a dark look at Bertie. "Oh! Well, it was my son's idea, really," she said. "He's the creative one in the family."

"I've never been so embarrassed in my entire life," Mom complained on the drive home. "Mrs. Nunley looked like she was going to explode."

Bertie couldn't understand what she was complaining about. After all, she wanted to win a prize, and she had.

You'd think she'd be grateful! Bertie thought. Everything had worked out pretty well, all in all. His mom had won a gardening kit, which included a large pair of green gardening gloves. Bertie was wearing them now. They were perfect for a garbage man.

When he was young, **Alan MacDonald** dreamed of becoming a professional soccer player, but when he

won a pen in a writing competition, his fate was sealed. Alan is now a successful author and television writer and has written several award-winning children's books, which have been translated into many languages.

David Roberts worked as a fashion illustrator in Hong Kong before turning to children's books. He has worked with a long list of writers, including Philip Ardagh, Georgia Byng, Carol Ann Duffy, and Chris Priestley. David has also won a gold award in the Nestle Children's Book Prize for *Mouse Noses on Toast* in 2006, and was shortlisted for the 2010 CILIP Kate Greenaway Medal for *The Dunderheads*.

Read more about Bertie at capstonekids.com/characters/dirty-bertie

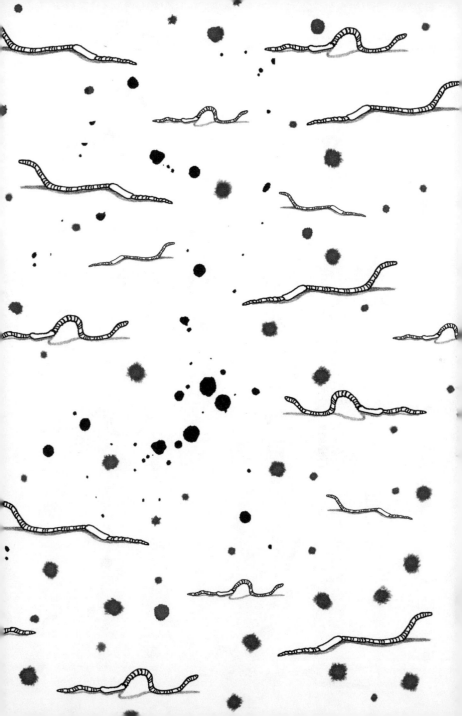

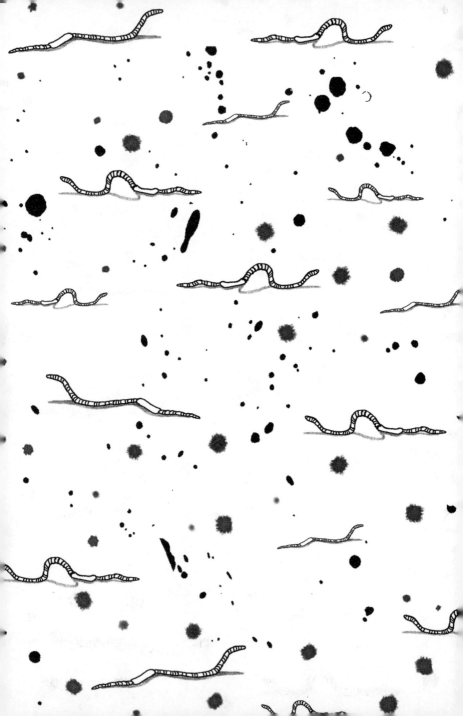